BUT AT LEAST I CAN TRY.

AND I'll TALK

IF I USE
ENOUGH
GLUE.

I CAN
PUT
THEM
AWAY.

I CAN REACH THE TOP SHELF.

Copyright © 2013 by Jeff Mack
A Neal Porter Book
Published by Roaring Brook Press
Roaring Brook Press is a division of Holtzbrinck
Publishing Holdings Limited Partnership
175 Fifth Avenue, New York, New York 10010
mackids.com

Library of Congress Cataloging-in-Publication Data
Mack, Jeff.
    The things I can do / Jeff Mack. — 1st ed.
        p. cm.
    "A Neal Porter Book."
    Summary: A boy shows a book he has made about all of
the things he can do for himself, from making his own
lunch to fixing his own toys.
    ISBN 978-1-59643-675-6 (hardcover)
[1. Stories in rhyme. 2. Ability—Fiction. 3. Books and
reading—Fiction.] I. Title.
    PZ8.3.M1747Hus 2013
    [E]—dc23
                                            2012012990

Roaring Brook Press books are available for special
promotions and premiums. For details contact: Director
of Special Markets, Holtzbrinck Publishers.

First edition 2013
Printed in China by Macmillan Production (Asia) Ltd.,
Kowloon Bay, Hong Kong (supplier code 10)
10 9 8 7 6 5 4 3 2 1

FOR OW.,
G. WOLF,
AND WNNY.